THE LAND
Peek-a-Boo.

By Roz Rosenbluth
Illustrated by Ben Mahan

© 1993 McClanahan Book Company, Inc. All rights reserved.
Published by McClanahan Book Company, Inc.
23 West 26th Street, New York, NY 10010

Printed in the U.S.A.

ISBN 1-56293-344-2

Tina loved to play Peek-A-Boo. She jumped out of the broom closet and yelled, "Peek-A-Boo," at her little brother Timmy.

"You scared me!" said Timmy. "Stop doing that."

"I like to play Peek-A-Boo," said Tina, and off she went to find another hiding place.

Tina jumped out of the toy chest.
"Peek-A-Boo!" she yelled at Timmy.

"Stop it," said Timmy. "You scared me!"
"That's the fun part," said Tina.

"It's no fun for me," said Timmy. "Let's play something else. How about playing hide and seek?"

"No," said Tina. "I like to play Peek-A-Boo." And off she went to find another hiding place.

That night Tina dreamed she was
walking along a road she had never seen before.
Suddenly she came to a big sign that said
The Land of Peek-A-Boo—This Way.

"That should be fun," thought Tina and she
started running in the direction of the arrow.

Soon she came to a forest thick with fir trees.

"Anyone here?" she called out.

Suddenly a deep voice yelled, "Peek-A-Boo!"

Tina jumped and looked up. A boy with red hair was sitting in the top branches of a fir tree.

"I see you," said Tina, but the boy disappeared into the tree tops.

Tina walked into town. There were shops
and little crooked streets, but no people.

"Where is everybody?" Tina called out.

"Peek-A-Boo," whispered a voice
right in back of her.

Tina whirled around and saw a blue skirt
disappearing around the corner. But when she
ran to the corner, nobody was there.

"Wait," Tina called out. "I want to play,
too." But no one answered.

She sat down on a bench and wondered what to do.

"Peek-A-Boo," said a voice right under her feet, and a little boy scampered out from under the bench and ran away.

"You scared me," Tina called after the boy. "That wasn't very nice. Why don't you stay and talk to me?"

"Oh, no," said the boy. "All we can do is play Peek-A-Boo. I must find another hiding place."

Tina opened the door of the bakery shop
and went in, but no one was there to wait on her.
Her mouth watered when she saw the bread and
rolls, and her eyes opened wide at the sight of a
huge cake with seven layers that went from the
floor to the ceiling.

Now, who could eat
all that cake, she wondered,
when suddenly a little girl
leaped out of the fifth layer
and cried out, "Peek-A-Boo!"

Tina ran out of the shop. All around her
voices were laughing and calling out, "Peek-A-
Boo! Peek-A-Boo!"

"Isn't this fun?" someone said to her.

"It's no fun for me," said Tina. "I never
know when anyone is going to jump out at me.
It's scary."

"Peek-A-Boo!" called a voice from behind a bush. "Peek-A-Boo! Peek-A-Boo!"

"Can't anyone here play anything else?" asked Tina. But all she could hear was "Peek-A-Boo! Peek-A-Boo!"

Tina closed her eyes and put her hands over her ears.

All of a sudden the voices stopped and Tina woke up in her own bed. She lay quietly thinking about her dream.

Then Tina went into Timmy's room and
gently shook his shoulder under the blanket.

"I just wanted to tell you that I will never
scare you with Peek-A-Boo again," she said.
"And I will only play it when you want to play."

Timmy poked his head from under the covers and smiled.

"Peek-A-Boo," he said.